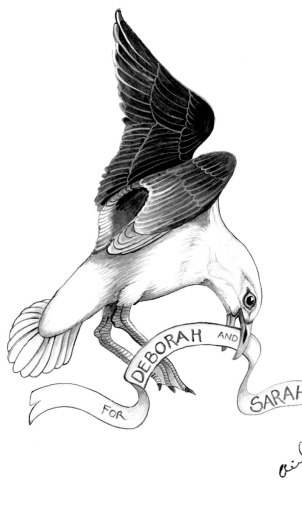

FOR DEBORAH AND SARAH

Music Street Press
Post Office Box 51, West Tisbury, MA 02575 USA

Book Design by Deborah J. Mayhew and Sarah L. Mayhew
drdeb@vineyard.net, slmayhew77@gmail.com

ISBN: 978-0692740095
0692740090

ISLANDER

The Circus Comes to Martha's Vineyard

By
Shirley W. Mayhew

Illustrated By
Linda Carnegie

MARTHA'S VINEYARD

Once upon a time - really, only a little while ago -
there was a ferry boat named Islander.

She was named Islander because every day she sailed
from a small town called Woods Hole,
in the state of Massachusetts,
out through the harbor,
into the body of water called Vineyard Sound,
and across to the island of Martha's Vineyard.

On each trip to Martha's Vineyard, Islander carried many things
that the people on the island needed -
fruits and vegetables to eat,
coats and overshoes to wear,
wood and bricks to build their houses with,
and newspapers and mail to read.

She carried chairs and tables to put into their houses,
milk and juice to drink,
pens and pencils and scotch tape to work with,
movies and television sets to watch,
and toys and games to play.

She brought books and magazines and radios,
and hot dogs and pet dogs and cats and goldfish
and toothbrushes and medicine.

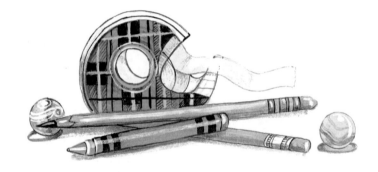

And she brought people.

In the winter Islander carried island people
   who had gone away to visit friends and relatives and cities.

And in the summer she brought off-island people
   who wanted to visit Martha's Vineyard.

Many, many people wanted to visit the island in the summer,
      and Islander was kept very busy sailing back to Woods Hole
         to bring more people to the island -
            big people, little people, fat people, thin people -
            and the people's cars and their luggage
               and their dogs and their grandmothers
               and their bicycles and their cats
               and their motor bikes.

Oh yes, Islander was kept very busy in the summertime,
      just like the island people who were kept very busy
         taking care of all those summer visitors.

And some days Islander got very tired of all those
   people and dogs and automobiles.

And some days the people got very tired of Islander,
      especially when she broke down
            on the Fourth of July weekend or Labor Day weekend
                  when even MORE people wanted to visit the island.

Every year Islander got more tired and slower
      and the people said,

      "We need a bigger boat to take us to the island."

And one day a brand new ferry boat arrived in Woods Hole
to help Islander take the people across the water.

Her name was Nantucket,
    because not only did she take people to Martha's Vineyard,
        but every day she went even farther out into the ocean
            and took people to another island called Nantucket.

Nantucket carried about 500 more people than did Islander.
    She was very proud and blew her whistle loudly.

Nantucket was a fine new boat with red leather seats
        and a lunch counter where you could buy
            hot dogs and Pepsi colas.

She had round tables you could eat on,
        and a big deck to walk on.

The people liked Nantucket better
        because they thought she was more comfortable.

But Woods Hole was very crowded in the summertime
with all the people and the cars,
and it still took 45 minutes to get to the Vineyard,
and the people said,

"This is very nice but we must get to the island faster."

And one day a shiny new double-ended ferry boat named Uncatena
arrived in Woods Hole to help Islander and Nantucket
carry the people and the freight across the water.

Uncatena was smaller than Islander but she had hydraulic doors
and could go very fast -15 knots per hour -
and it took only thirty minutes to reach the Vineyard.

Uncatena was very grand with her green deck chairs
and the white, foamy water streaming out behind her
as she raced toward the island.

Poor Islander felt quite old and slow and ugly
when she lay at the dock
between Nantucket and Uncatena in Woods Hole.

Every day Islander chugged along carrying people and supplies to the island,
and Nantucket passed her with flags flying on her way to Nantucket,
and Uncatena passed her on her way back to Woods Hole,
and Islander rocked in the waves caused by the other boats.

She grew very sad and went even slower.

Finally one day, early in the summer, Islander burned out a piston,
which meant she couldn't sail to Martha's Vineyard
until it was fixed.

But it was late June and no-one had time to fix it,
as they were all so busy running Nantucket and Uncatena
back and forth to the islands.

Pretty soon everyone forgot poor Islander,
and as the summer grew hotter
she could hear the happy chatter of the people
and the laughter of the children
as the visitors piled aboard the other ferries
for their voyage across Vineyard Sound.

Islander wept great salt tears into the harbor,
and heaved great sighs that made her planks rattle.

She was truly sad because she thought no-one
would ever stand on her decks again
and watch the spray fly and the seagulls soar.

And so the month of July went by
and Islander's paint began to peel,
and barnacles grew on her hull.

But wait - who is that man
with the tall black hat and boots standing on the dock?

He is talking to the men who run the boats,
and he is saying,

"I want to take my circus to Martha's Vineyard,
because many of the children there
have never seen a real circus.

But I will need a big, wide boat because my circus has
one lion,
two tigers,
four camels,
six horses,
ten monkeys,
and eight elephants.

And I will need a slow, steady boat
so that my animals will not be tossed around and get seasick.

Do you have such a boat?"

The men who run the boats looked around -
  there was the sleek Nantucket, standing high in the water
    and looking very proud and haughty.

She didn't want camels and horses prancing around
  marking up her deck, and she didn't want monkeys
    playing on her shiny, red leather chairs.

Nantucket tried to shrink back behind the big freight shed
  so that she wouldn't be noticed.

And there was speedy little Uncatena -
  the very thought of those eight heavy elephants on her deck
    made her shudder and shake,
      and she tried to hide behind Islander.

And finally, there was old Islander -
  big and very wide, slow but very steady.

Islander had listened carefully
when she heard the man talking about his circus,
and the thought of taking a circus
to the island children made her very happy.

She tried to stand tall and big alongside the dock,
and she did everything but blow her whistle
to make the man notice her.

The men walked over to Nantucket, and the circus man said,

"She is a beautiful boat, but my animals would be frightened
at all those shiny, red seats,
and she does look kind of top-heavy."

Then they walked over to Uncatena trembling at the dockside,
and the circus man said,
"She is a lovely boat, but she is too small -
my elephants might sink her.

Don't you have another boat?"

Then the circus man noticed Islander and walked over to look at her.

He said, "This boat looks old and tired,
  but she is big and wide and won't go too fast -
    she looks just right for my circus."

Islander was so happy that she almost leaped out of the water with joy.
  She let out a short toot on her whistle,
    and almost broke one of her dock lines in her excitement.
      Then the men went away to make the arrangements
        for the circus to go to Martha's Vineyard.

The next day some workmen arrived and went aboard Islander
  to get her ready to carry the circus.
    For the next two weeks ten men worked hard on Islander;
      they repaired her burned-out piston,
        they cleared the lower deck and built stalls
          for the elephants and camels and horses,
            and they cleared large spaces for the trucks
              that would carry the lions
                and tigers and monkeys.

They scraped the barnacles off of Islander's hull, and painted the decks and doors, and cleaned the deck chairs for the clowns and other performers to sit on, and they even polished the brass.

When they were all finished, Islander just gleamed - she looked like a new boat. And she was happy - SO happy. For two days she sat at the dock in anticipation.

And finally, one afternoon in early August,
   the circus trucks began rolling into Woods Hole.
      Islander moved into the ferry slip and opened her wide doors.
         First to go aboard were the trucks carrying the lions and tigers,
            and Islander could hear them roaring, but she wasn't afraid.
            Then came the trucks with the monkeys and parrots
               and smaller animals like the trick dogs.

And last, but not least, came the big animals.

When the trucks were all in place,
    six white horses came prancing and dancing
      and made clickety-clackety noises
       as they trotted onto the boat.

Following them came four haughty camels,
    stepping carefully over the gangplank
      and walking sedately onto Islander's lower deck.

Finally, not four, not six, but eight elephants

(seven huge ones and one baby)

swaying slowly from side to side,

lumbered onto the creaking gang-plank

and stepped cautiously into Islander,

who slowly settled a little deeper into the water.

At last they were all set to sail to Martha's Vineyard.

Islander's two diesel engines turned over,
and her planks creaked as she prepared to leave for the Vineyard.

First she drew in her stern line,
and then she drew in her two cable lines,
and as she slowly pulled away from the ferry slip in Woods Hole,
she gave a happy little toot on her whistle.

Carefully she moved out into the harbor,
tooting at the small sailboats and fishing draggers
to get out of her way, and gently she fought the tide
as she left the harbor and went out into Vineyard Sound.

When she was finally out in open water,
she gave a happy little sigh and speeded up her engines.

The afternoon was sunny, and the water had little ripples on it.
Islander's fresh paint glistened,
and without the barnacles on her hull,
she fairly skimmed over the water. Before she knew it,
the 45 minute trip was almost over.

As she slowed down her engines and approached the breakwater,
Islander saw a fleet of small boats
within the entrance to the Vineyard harbor.

When she gave a warning toot, they all began to circle her.

And as they got closer Islander saw
that they were filled with Island children -
and even some Island grown-ups.

The small boats quickly surrounded Islander,
and the children, laughing and cheering,
waved to Islander and the circus animals.

The camels smiled, the horses whinnied,
the monkeys ran up and down Islander's smokestack,
and the elephants raised their trunks and trumpeted.

Everyone was so happy and proud of Islander
for bringing the circus
to the children of Martha's Vineyard.

And after the circus had left the Vineyard,
    all the people loved Islander
        and wanted to ride on her wide deck to the Vineyard
            so that they could say,

"I rode on the ferry that brought the circus to Martha's Vineyard."

THE END

ABOUT THE STORY

This story is fiction based on an event that really happened. In August of 1963 a real circus came to Martha's Vineyard and gave two performances at Waban Park in the town of Oak Bluffs.

A traveling circus usually traveled from town to town by train or on trucks – this was the first circus ever to transport its animals, people, and supplies across a body of water to an island seven miles off the coast of Massachusetts.

Ferry boats make daily trips to Martha's Vineyard bringing supplies to the island as well as people and cars and trucks, an occasional pet dog, and perhaps two or three riding horses in a horse van. But never had they carried lions and tigers and elephants – or the entire makings of a circus. After about a year of planning, it took two of the ferry boats six round trips in the middle of the night to transport the entire circus to the Vineyard. It was an exciting affair and attracted about 6,000 people, some from Cape Cod and Nantucket.

The Mills Brothers Circus gave two performances on August 5, 1963 in Oak Bluffs on Martha's Vineyard, and came back to the Vineyard in 1965 to perform in Edgartown.

Photo by Howell's Photo Studio
published in the Vineyard Gazette Aug. 3, 1965

Photo courtesy of David Chickering

Photo courtesy of Arthur W. Young, Jr.

Photo courtesy of David Chickering

ABOUT THE AUTHOR AND ILLUSTRATOR

Photo courtesy of
Lynn Christoffers

Shirley W. Mayhew. I arrived on Martha's Vineyard in 1947 as a 21 year old bride, after studying at Brown University for three years. I married an Islander, and my husband John and I built a home and raised a son and two daughters in West Tisbury. A photographer since childhood, I recorded the life of my children – and later my three granddaughters – as they grew up. While my own children were still young, I worked as a freelance photographer, specializing in portraits of children.

Married in an era of "stay at home Moms", I finally finished college at the age of thirty-eight, got my first full-time job at the age of forty, and for twenty years taught Language Arts to grades 6, 7, and 8 at the Edgartown School. After my children were grown, I turned to painting in water colors, traveling the world, and finally, to writing.

Islander is the third book I have published. In 1973 I published Seasons of a Vineyard Pond, a one year journal of the wildlife in and around Look's Pond in West Tisbury, which I wrote as a Bachelor's degree thesis and illustrated myself; in 2014 I gathered about forty of my essays with accompanying photographs, and self-published them under the title Looking Back: My Long Life on Martha's Vineyard.

Now, at 90 and after thirty years of retirement, I am still writing, but no longer photographing, painting, traveling – or riding my bike.

Linda Carnegie. I washed ashore on the Vineyard in 1974 and have been painting ever since. Clients have included Mass General Hospital for Children in Boston, MA, Rainbow Babies and Children's Hospital in Cleveland, OH, and the wonderful West Tisbury Library here on the Vineyard.

This book is dedicated to my new friend Shirley and all my dear friends and family who help me stumble through this life adventure. And to my heart, my son Jonah who is my sun. ☀

http://www.lindacarnegiedesigns.com/

Photo by Mark Lovewell
courtesy of the
Vineyard Gazette

AUTHOR'S ACKNOWLEDGMENTS

So many thanks to Linda Carnegie for her delightful illustrations.

And to my two daughters, Deborah and Sarah, who designed and produced this book when I finally got too old to cope with the computer skills it required.

And finally, thanks to Cliff Lenox on Cape Cod whose idea it was to bring the circus to Martha's Vineyard more than fifty years ago.